Pipsqueaks Maze School
right this way.
Lots of mazes
every day!

Are you ready
to begin?
There's the school bell.
Let's go in!

Attention, maze solvers.
You can do all these mazes
by pointing with your finger.

Drop Off

Cars and buses
are arriving.
To the entrance
we are driving.

Our first day
there's lots to learn—
First thing is
to wait your turn.

There are many Pipsqueaks being dropped off at Maze School.
Can you figure out which road leads to the entrance?

PIPSQUEAKS!

MAZE SCHOOL

Written and Illustrated by
Patrick Merrell

Cartwheel
B·O·O·K·S®
SCHOLASTIC INC.
New York   Toronto   London   Auckland   Sydney

Dedicated to:
Sharon Singer
Steve Metzger

ISBN 0-590-03712-9

Copyright © 1998 by Patrick Merrell.
Book design by Patrick Merrell.
Pipsqueaks name, logo, and characters
are a trademark of Patrick Merrell.
SCHOLASTIC, CARTWHEEL BOOKS and the CARTWHEEL BOOKS logo
are trademarks and/or registered trademarks of Scholastic Inc.
All rights reserved. Published by Scholastic Inc.

12 11 10 9 8 7 6 5 4 3 2   9/9 0/0 01 02
Printed in the U.S.A.   24
First printing, September 1998

Tile Time

Down the hallway
we all scurry.
To our classroom,
come on, hurry!

Colored tiles
lead the way.
To the doorway,
do not stray.

There are mazes everywhere in Maze School.
Stepping only on purple tiles, can you find a route that
will lead us to our classroom door?

Block Party

Lifting, loading
from the box.
Sorting, stacking
building blocks.

Build a tower,
build a rocket.
Please be careful
not to knock it.

Can you find a way through this maze of blocks
from the skyscraper to the rocket ship?

Brush Up

Here's some paper,
take a brush.
Lots to choose from,
there's no rush.

Paint your paper,
make a maze.
Many colors,
many ways.

We have painted eight small mazes.
We have taped them together to make one large maze.
Can you follow the entire length of this colorful path?

Snack Attack

For our snack
there's milk and juice.
Lots of straws here
for our use.

We can drink milk
anywhere.
Juice that's here,
we drink from there.

We have stuck our straws together.
Can you figure out which Pipsqueak is drinking which drink?

Race and Chase

On your marks now,
take your places.
Get in line
for classroom races.

Turtle, frog,
and rabbit, too.
Which of them
will make it through?

Only one of these classroom animals is going to make it
through this maze of chalkboard erasers to the finish line.
Can you figure out which one?

Start

Start

Start

End!

Entries:
• Fluffy
• Shelly
• Legs

Playground Pipsqueaks

It's our favorite
time of day.
Time to go
outside and play!

Let's all follow—
there's the leader.
Follow closely,
to the feeder!

Starting below, can you follow this line of
Pipsqueaks to the leader at the bird feeder?

Start

End!

Mountain Fountain

5, 4, 3, 2, 1
we're countin'.
Thar she blows—
a bubbling mountain!

Fizzing foam
flows from its spout.
Down its sides
the suds spill out.

We made our volcano by adding vinegar to baking soda.
Can you find the path of bubbling "lava" that flows all the
way to the "lake" we painted in the corner of the box?

Ants Dance

Ants are crawling
up and down.
Ants are digging
underground.

One ant's lost
outside the nest.
Can you help him
join the rest?

Can you help the one ant at the top get
down to the queen's chamber at the bottom?

Start

END

Rest
Test

Pipsqueaks sitting
on the floor.
Blankets laid out
door to door.

While some read
or draw or rest,
others do
this blanket test.

No resting for you.
Without stepping on any blankets,
can you find a way from door to door?

Sand Blast

Using cups and pots
and spoons,
we have built
a maze of dunes.

Help us travel
in between,
through this sandy
desert scene.

Traveling in the paths between the high rows of sand,
can you find a way for us to get to the oasis?

Start

End!

Hamster Scamper

We have helped
our hamster friends
build a home
of twists and bends.

In the tubes
we crawl and play.
Oops, a dead end —
not this way!

There is more than one way to get through this tube town
to the hamster wheel. How many ways can you find?

Trip Trap

We are going
on a bus,
on a school trip,
all of us.

We could use
a school trip guide.
Come and join us
on our ride.

We are going on a field trip.
Where? To a field!
Can you help us get there?

How to Make a SCHOOL MAZE

Here's a fun and easy maze you can make by yourself or with some friends.

Cut 2 – 6 squares of paper.
About 8" x 8" is a good size.

Make a pencil mark in
the middle of each side.

If you are making a maze with friends,
each person gets one square.
If you are making a maze alone, give yourself all the squares.

Draw a maze on each piece of paper. The maze must start at one of the four marks on the paper. It must end up at **only one** of the other three marks.

Collect all the papers. Arrange them like a jigsaw puzzle so that the starting and ending points match up.
Add a piece that says "Start" and one that says "End" and your maze is ready to solve!

Chalk
Talk

Go back now
and closely gaze.
A box of chalk
is in each maze.

When you see it,
you must squawk.
Speak right up
and holler, "Chalk!"

CHALK!

There is one box of chalk hiding in every maze.
Can you find each one?